by
Chelsey Luciow

CAPSTONE PRESS
a capstone imprint

Dabble Lab is published by Capstone Press, an imprint of Capstone.
1710 Roe Crest Drive, North Mankato, Minnesota 56003
capstonepub.com

Copyright © 2025 by Capstone. All rights reserved. No part of this publication may be reproduced in whole or in part, or stored in a retrieval system, or transmitted in any form or by any means, electronic, mechanical, photocopying, recording, or otherwise, without written permission of the publisher.

Library of Congress Cataloging-in-Publication Data is available on the Library of Congress website.
ISBN: 9781669093190 (hardcover)
ISBN: 9781669093152 (ebook PDF)

Summary: Get a taste of the world when you cook up treats across cultures! From Samoan coconut buns to Somali mango shakes to Irish sausage rolls, these easy-to-make recipes are sure to satisfy your snack-time cravings.

Image Credits: Adobe Stock: donatas1205, 12 (background), Obsessively, 16 (background); Mighty Media, Inc. (project photos)
Design Elements: Adobe Stock: byMechul, zhaluldesign; Mighty Media, Inc.

Editorial Credits
Editor: Jessica Rusick
Designer: Denise Hamernik

Any additional websites and resources referenced in this book are not maintained, authorized, or sponsored by Capstone. All product and company names are trademarks™ or registered® trademarks of their respective holders.

The publisher and the author shall not be liable for any damages allegedly arising from the information in this book, and they specifically disclaim any liability from the use or application of any of the contents of this book.

Printed and bound in China. 6096

Table of Contents

Cooking Up Treats 4
French Chocolate Baguette 6
Ukrainian Sweet Cheese Tarts 9
Venezuelan Guasacaca 10
Irish Sausage Rolls 13
Mexican Atole with Banana 14
Samoan Coconut Buns 17
New Zealand Meat Pies 18
Palestinian Mutabbaq 21
German Pfeffernüsse Cookies 22
Somali Mango Milkshake 25
Marshallese Baked Papaya 26
Cameroonian Candied Groundnuts 29
Portuguese Serradura Pudding 30
    Read More 32
    Internet Sites 32
    About the Author 32

Cooking Up TREATS

Kids in countries around the world eat all kinds of treats between and after meals. Whether sweet or savory, many meals are beloved dishes in the cultures they come from. Make Samoan coconut buns, Ukrainian cheese tarts, Portuguese pudding, and more to experience foods from many cultures!

Basic Supplies

- baking sheet
- blender
- frying pan
- knife and cutting board
- measuring cups and spoons
- mixing bowls
- parchment paper
- rolling pin
- spatula
- whisk

Kitchen Tips

1. Ask an adult for permission before you make a recipe.

2. Ask an adult for help when using a knife, blender, grater, stove, or oven. Wear oven mitts when removing items from the oven or microwave.

3. Read through the recipe and set out all ingredients and supplies before you start working.

4. Using metric tools? Use the conversion chart on the right to make your recipe measure up.

5. Wash your hands before and after you handle food. Wash and dry fresh produce before use.

6. When you are done making food, clean your work surface and wash dirty dishes. Put all supplies and ingredients back where you found them.

Standard	Metric
¼ teaspoon	1.25 grams or milliliters
½ teaspoon	2.5 g or mL
1 teaspoon	5 g or mL
1 tablespoon	15 g or mL
¼ cup	57 g (dry) or 60 mL (liquid)
⅓ cup	75 g (dry) or 80 mL (liquid)
½ cup	114 g (dry) or 125 mL (liquid)
⅔ cup	150 g (dry) or 160 mL (liquid)
¾ cup	170 g (dry) or 175 mL (liquid)
1 cup	227 g (dry) or 240 mL (liquid)
1 quart	950 mL

French Chocolate Baguette

French children commonly eat this sweet, simple treat during le goûter (luh GOO-teh). This is a special snack time that takes place after school and before dinner.

Ingredients
(makes 4 servings)

- 1 baguette
- 1 stick room temperature salted butter
- 1 milk chocolate bar

1. Cut the baguette in half lengthwise with a bread knife. Cut each half into four slices.
2. Butter all of the baguette slices generously.
3. Break the chocolate bar into pieces. Place the chocolate bar pieces onto the baguette slices.
4. Place a buttered baguette slice on top of each chocolate slice to make four sandwiches.

Chocolate Bread

Pain au chocolat (PEHN oh shock-oh-LAH) is a similar French treat made with flaky pastry. The name means "chocolate bread."

Ukrainian Sweet Cheese Tarts

This sweet cheese dish is similar to cheesecake! It is commonly served as a dessert or side dish during Easter.

Ingredients
(makes 18 to 24 tarts)

- 6 cups dry cottage cheese (also called farmer's cheese)
- 7 eggs
- ½ cup sugar
- 1 teaspoon vanilla extract
- fruit jams or fresh fruit pieces for toppings

1. Preheat the oven to 390 degrees Fahrenheit (200 degrees Celsius). Grease a 24-cup mini muffin tin.
2. Mix together the cheese, eggs, sugar, and vanilla extract in a large bowl.
3. Scoop about ⅓ cup of the cheese mixture into each cup of the muffin tin.
4. Bake the tarts for 25 minutes or until the tops are firm and the edges are golden.
5. Let the tarts cool for 10 minutes in the muffin tin. Then remove the tarts and place them on a wire rack to finish cooling.
6. Once cooled, place the tarts on a serving plate. Add fruit jam or fresh fruit to the top of each tart. If you'd like, use a mini cookie cutter to cut the fruit into shapes.

Syrnyk
In Ukraine, sweet Easter cheese is called syrnyk (SIR-nick).

Venezuelan Guasacaca

Guasacaca (gwah-sah-CAH-cah) is served as a dip and a condiment. It is sometimes called Venezuelan guacamole.

Ingredients
(makes 6 servings)

- 2 ripe avocados
- 1 onion, chopped
- 2 green peppers, chopped
- 2 cloves garlic
- ½ bunch fresh parsley
- ½ bunch fresh cilantro
- ⅓ cup red wine vinegar
- 1 tablespoon salt
- ¼ teaspoon pepper
- 1 cup olive oil
- crackers or tortilla chips

1. Cut the avocados in half and remove the pits. Scoop the flesh into a food processor. Add the onion, green pepper, garlic, parsley, cilantro, vinegar, salt, and pepper. Blend until almost smooth.

2. Add the oil in a slow stream while the food processor runs at low speed. Keep blending until the oil is fully mixed in.

3. Let the guasacaca sit at room temperature for at least 1 hour. Taste it and add more salt and pepper if desired.

4. Pour the guasacaca into a bowl and serve it at room temperature with crackers or tortilla chips for dipping. If made ahead of time, store the dip in a covered container in the refrigerator and bring it to room temperature before serving.

Enjoy!
Say "buen provecho" (BWEN proh-VEH-cho) before serving this dish. It means "enjoy" in Spanish, Venezuela's official language.

Say Sausage
In Irish, the word *ispín* (ISH-peen) means "sausage."

Irish Sausage Rolls

These comforting treats have been popular in Ireland since the 1800s. They are sold at bakeries and pubs throughout the country.

Ingredients
(makes about 18 rolls)

- 1 pound ground sausage
- 1 large egg
- 1 small onion, finely chopped
- ¾ cup fresh breadcrumbs
- ½ teaspoon salt
- ½ teaspoon pepper
- 1 puff pastry sheet

1. Preheat the oven to 375°F (190°C). Line a baking sheet with parchment paper.
2. Mix the sausage, egg, onion, breadcrumbs, salt, and pepper together in a bowl. Set the bowl aside.
3. Whisk the egg in a small bowl. Set the bowl aside.
4. Lightly flour a surface and roll out the pastry sheet into a 12-by-14-inch (30-by-35-centimeter) rectangle. Cut the rectangle in half lengthwise into two long strips.
5. Scoop half the sausage filling onto a pastry strip. The filling should be in a line running down the center of the strip. Leave at least 1 inch (2.5 cm) between the filling and the sides of the pastry. Brush the edges of the pastry with the egg.
6. Fold one long side of the pastry over the filling to meet the pastry's other long side. Seal the edge by pressing a fork along its length.
7. Repeat steps 5 and 6 with the other pastry strip to make a second sausage log.
8. Use a fork to poke small holes in the top of each log.
9. Cut each log into pieces about 1½ inches (4 cm) long. Place the sausage rolls on the baking sheet. Brush the top of each one with egg wash.
10. Bake the sausage rolls for 35 to 40 minutes or until they are golden brown and puffy. Let them cool for 15 minutes before serving.

Mexican Atole with Banana

Atole (ah-TOH-lay) is a sweet drink commonly served during the Day of the Dead and the Christmas season. The earliest versions date back thousands of years!

Ingredients
(makes 2 servings)

- 1 cup water
- 1 cup regular milk, almond milk, or soy milk
- 1 ripe banana, sliced
- ¼ cup blue corn flour (can substitute yellow or white corn flour)
- ⅛ teaspoon cinnamon
- ⅛ teaspoon ground cardamom
- ½ teaspoon vanilla extract
- maple syrup to taste

1. Blend the water, milk, and banana in a blender until smooth. Pour the mixture into a saucepan.

2. Heat the pan over medium heat. Whisk in the corn flour when the liquid begins to steam. Heat the mixture until small bubbles form. Then stir in the cinnamon, cardamom, and vanilla extract. Add maple syrup 1 teaspoon at a time until the atole is as sweet as you'd like.

3. Bring the atole to a boil, stirring constantly. Reduce the heat to low and continue stirring for 2 to 3 minutes to avoid lumps.

4. Pour the atole into mugs and top it with cinnamon if you'd like. Let it cool for a few minutes before drinking.

Masa

Mexican atole is usually made with masa (MAH-sah). This traditional ground corn flour is also used to make tortillas, tamales, and more.

Samoan Coconut Buns

Coconut buns are often served at family gatherings in Samoa. The buns are one of Samoa's national dishes!

Ingredients
(makes 12 buns)

- 12 frozen dinner rolls
- 1 cup sugar
- 13.5-ounce can coconut milk
- 1 teaspoon vanilla extract

1. Preheat the oven to 350°F (180°C). Grease a 9-by-13-inch (23-by-33-cm) baking dish. Place the rolls into the dish so they are evenly spaced. Cover them with a clean kitchen towel and set them aside to rise.

2. Mix together the sugar, coconut milk, and vanilla extract in a large bowl.

3. Uncover the rolls. Pour about three-quarters of the coconut mixture over them.

4. Bake the rolls for 20 to 25 minutes or until they are golden brown.

5. Pour the remaining coconut mixture over the buns while they are warm. Serve them right away. Freeze leftovers in an airtight container and thaw them in the refrigerator when you're ready to eat. Bake the buns at 350°F (180°C) for 5 minutes to warm them up.

Pani Popo
In Samoan, coconut buns are called pani popo (PAH-nee POH-poh). *Pani* means "bun," and *popo* means "coconut."

New Zealand Meat Pies

British colonists popularized meat pies in the 1800s. Now they are a staple in New Zealand bakeries. The country even holds an annual contest to find the best pies!

Ingredients
(makes 12 mini pies)

- 1 teaspoon olive oil
- 2 strips bacon, finely chopped
- ½ small red onion, diced
- 4 eggs
- ½ cup whole milk
- ¾ cup grated sharp cheddar cheese
- ½ teaspoon salt
- ½ teaspoon pepper
- 1 to 2 sheets puff pastry, enough for twelve 3-inch (7.6-cm) circles

1. Preheat the oven to 375°F (190°C). Grease a 12-cup mini muffin tin.
2. Heat the olive oil in a frying pan over medium-high heat. Add the bacon and onion. Cook until the onion is translucent and the bacon begins to brown, about 7 minutes. Spoon the mixture onto a plate lined with paper towels. Set the plate aside.
3. Mix together the eggs, milk, cheese, salt, and pepper in a bowl.
4. Lightly flour a flat surface. Roll the pastry so it is ½ inch (1.3 cm) thick. Use a 3-inch (7.6-cm) cookie cutter or glass rim to cut 12 pastry circles. Press each circle into a muffin tin compartment to form pastry cups.
5. Fill each cup about three-fourths full with the egg mixture. Sprinkle the bacon and onion mixture on top.
6. Bake the meat pies in the oven for 15 to 20 minutes or until they are golden brown. Let them cool for 5 minutes before serving.

Many Fillings
New Zealand's meat pies come in many flavors, including chicken and seafood. Some also contain kumara (KOO-mah-rah), another word for "sweet potato."

Mutabbaq Meaning
Mutabbaq (moo-TAH-bahk) is an Arabic word. It means "folded."

Palestinian Mutabbaq

People in Palestine have been eating these sweet cheese pastries for hundreds of years. They are famous for their many layers of thin, crispy dough.

Ingredients
(makes 6 pastries)

- 1 cup plus 1 tablespoon sugar
- 1 cup water
- ⅛ teaspoon orange extract
- 2 teaspoons lemon juice
- 10½ ounces fresh mozzarella cheese
- ½ sheet puff pastry
- 4 tablespoons butter, melted
- crushed pistachios (optional)

1. Make the sugar syrup. Heat 1 cup sugar and 1 cup water in a saucepan over medium-high heat. Bring the mixture to a low boil and cook for 2 to 3 minutes or until the sugar is fully dissolved. Stir in the orange extract and lemon juice. Set the pan aside.

2. Preheat the oven to 400°F (200°C). Grease a baking sheet.

3. Make the filling. Break the mozzarella into medium chunks in a bowl. Pat the cheese dry with paper towels. Mix in the 1 tablespoon sugar. Set the bowl aside.

4. Roll out the pastry on a lightly floured surface. Cut the sheet horizontally into three equal strips. Roll each strip into a rectangle about 7 by 13 inches (18 by 33 cm). Cut each rectangle in half to make two squares.

5. Roll each square so it has 7.5-inch (19-cm) sides. Brush each square with some of the butter. Spoon 3 tablespoons of filling in the middle of each square. Leave a 2-inch (5-cm) border around the filling.

6. Fold two opposite sides of each square over the filling. Then fold the other two sides over the filling. The pastries should look like little envelopes.

7. Place the pastries on the baking sheet and brush the tops with the remaining melted butter. Bake the pastries for 10 to 13 minutes or until they are golden brown. Pour the sugar syrup over the pastries when they come out of the oven. Sprinkle pistachios on top if you'd like.

German Pfeffernüsse Cookies

These spiced cookies are a common treat in Germany during Christmastime.

Ingredients
(makes 36 cookies)

- 1 cup sugar
- ½ cup butter
- ¼ cup buttermilk
- ¼ cup molasses
- 2¼ cups all-purpose flour
- 1 teaspoon baking soda
- ½ teaspoon ground ginger
- ½ teaspoon ground cinnamon
- ¼ teaspoon ground cloves
- ¼ teaspoon pepper
- powdered sugar

1. Use an electric mixer to combine the sugar, butter, buttermilk, and molasses in a large bowl.

2. Add the flour a little bit at a time and mix until it is just blended. Add the baking soda, ginger, cinnamon, cloves, and pepper and mix well.

3. Cover the dough with plastic wrap and refrigerate it for at least 2 hours. Chilling the dough makes it easier to work with.

4. Preheat the oven to 350°F (180°C). Divide the dough into four equal pieces on a floured surface. Shape each piece into a log about 15 inches (38 cm) long and 1 inch (2.5 cm) wide.

5. Cut the logs into ¼-inch (0.6-cm) slices with a serrated knife. Place the slices ¼ inch (0.6 cm) apart on an ungreased cookie sheet.

6. Bake the cookies for 8 to 9 minutes or until they are golden brown. Cool the cookies on a wire rack for 5 minutes. Then sprinkle on powdered sugar.

Peppernuts

Pfeffernüsse (FEH-fare-nooh-suh) means "peppernuts" in German. The name likely comes from the pepper and other spices in the dough.

Somali Mango Milkshake

People in Somalia drink mango milkshakes during hot summers and the fasting month of Ramadan.

Ingredients
(makes 2 servings)

- 5 ice cubes
- ¾ cup mango pulp (crushed mango)
- 1 cup milk
- 2 scoops vanilla ice cream
- ⅛ teaspoon salt
- 4 tablespoons strawberry jam
- ⅛ teaspoon cardamom powder

1. Place the serving glasses in the freezer. This will help make the milkshakes extra cold.
2. Blend the ice cubes, mango, milk, ice cream, and salt in a blender.
3. Spoon 2 tablespoons of strawberry jam into the bottom of each glass. Pour the milkshake on top. Sprinkle the cardamom on top and enjoy right away.

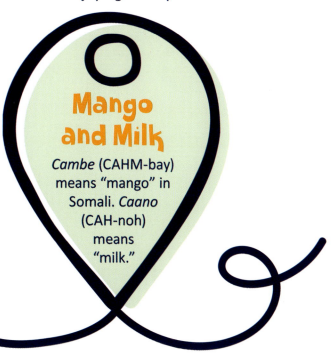

Mango and Milk
Cambe (CAHM-bay) means "mango" in Somali. *Caano* (CAH-noh) means "milk."

Marshallese Baked Papaya

Europeans likely introduced papaya to the Marshall Islands in the 1800s. Since then, the tropical fruit has become common in Marshallese dishes.

Ingredients
(makes 2 servings)

- 1 ripe papaya
- 4 tablespoons water
- 4 tablespoons sugar
- ½ cup coconut milk

1. Preheat the oven to 375°F (190°C). Cut the papaya in half lengthwise and scoop out the black seeds.

2. Place the papaya halves onto a baking sheet. Pour 2 tablespoons of water in each half. Then sprinkle 2 tablespoons of sugar over each half.

3. Bake the papaya for 45 minutes. Remove it from the oven and immediately pour ¼ cup coconut milk into each half. Wait about 5 minutes for the papaya to warm the coconut milk. Serve the dish right away.

Papaya and Coconut

"Papaya" is *keinabbu* (key-in-ah-boo) in Marshallese. "Coconut" is *ni* (NEE).

Cameroonian Candied Groundnuts

Candied groundnuts, or peanuts, are sold as a street food in Cameroon. They are traditionally made with only a few simple ingredients.

Ingredients
(makes 8 servings)

- 2 cups raw peanuts (groundnuts)
- 1 cup sugar
- ½ cup water
- ½ teaspoon salt
- ½ teaspoon nutmeg (optional)

1. Roast the peanuts in a skillet over medium heat for about 8 minutes, stirring occasionally.
2. Mix together the sugar, water, salt, and nutmeg (if using) in a pot over medium heat. Stir in the roasted peanuts. Bring the mixture to a bubble and keep stirring until the sugar crystallizes on the peanuts. This should take about 5 minutes.
3. Spread the groundnuts on a baking sheet to cool. Eat once cooled and store any leftovers in an airtight container.

Peanut Pronunciation

English and French are Cameroon's official languages. In French, "peanut" is *la cacahuète* (lah ka-ka-YEH-tah).

Portuguese Serradura Pudding

This dessert is sold in bakeries across Portugal. It is traditionally made with Maria cookies, a popular packaged cookie similar to a shortbread cookie.

Ingredients
(makes 1 to 2 servings)

- 30 shortbread cookies or tea biscuits
- 2 cups heavy whipping cream, cold
- ½ teaspoon vanilla
- 1 cup sweetened condensed milk
- toppings such as shredded coconut, slivered almonds, and passion fruit (optional)

1. Pulse the cookies in a food processor until they are finely crushed. You can also place the cookies in a resealable plastic bag and crush them with a rolling pin. Pour the crumbs into a bowl.

2. Pour the whipping cream into a bowl and add the vanilla. Use an electric mixer to beat the mixture on high for 30 seconds or until fluffy.

3. Add the condensed milk and continue to beat the mixture until stiff peaks form. Don't overbeat the mixture or it will become butter.

4. Sprinkle about ¼ cup cookie crumbs in the bottom of a glass. Then spoon about ¼ cup cream mixture on top. Continue layering until you reach the top of the glass, ending on a cream layer. If using small glasses, you should have enough for two puddings.

5. Cover the glass(es) with plastic wrap and refrigerate for at least 3 hours or overnight. If you'd like, top with coconut, almonds, passion fruit, or other favorite toppings before serving.

Read More

Gregory, Josh. *Pastry Chef.* Ann Arbor, MI: Cherry Lake Publishing, 2022.

Herrington, Lisa M. *Desserts Around the World.* New York: Scholastic, 2022.

Peterson, Tamara JM. *Snack Time Food Art.* North Mankato, MN: Capstone, 2024.

Internet Sites

Casdoce, a Confection Made for Lords & Emperors
thekidshouldseethis.com/post/making-kasudousu-casdoce-a-dessert-for-emperors

Food from Around the World Spotlight
pbs.org/video/food-from-around-the-world-spotlight-lsisge/

The Most Popular Snack in Countries Around the World
businessinsider.com/snacks-around-the-world-2017-7

About the Author

Chelsey Luciow is an artist and creator. She loves reading with kids and believes books are magical. Chelsey lives in Minneapolis with her wife, their son, and their dogs.